Home Sweet Home

Home Sweet Home

Jean Marzollo

ILLUSTRATED BY

Ashley Wolff

HARPERCOLLINS*PUBLISHERS*

Library of Congress Cataloging-in-Publication Data
Marzollo, Jean.
  Home sweet home / by Jean Marzollo; illustrated by Ashley Wolff.
    p.   cm.
  Summary: Illustrations and simple rhyming text ask blessings on everything on earth, from
ant to tree, stream to whale, and also on moonbeams and stars.
  ISBN 0-06-027562-6 — ISBN 0-06-027353-4 (lib. bdg.) — ISBN 0-06-443501-6 (pbk.)
  1. Earth—Religious aspects—Juvenile literature. 2. Children—Prayer-books and devo-
tions—English. [1. Prayers. 2. Earth—Religious aspects.] I. Wolff, Ashley, ill. II. Title.
BL438.2M37   1997   96-35410
291.4'3—dc20   CIP
                                                                                AC

Typography by Al Cetta
❖
Visit us on the World Wide Web!
http://www.harperchildrens.com

For Phoebe and Kirby
J. M.

For Jewell and Bud, with love
A.W.

Bless each bee

Each flower and tree

Each cloud in the sky

Each stalk of rye

Bless each hare

Each fish, each bear

Each tender calf

Each tall giraffe

Bless each wren

Each rooster and hen

Each turtle
and snake

Each duck and drake

Each dolphin and whale

Each little snail

Bless each foal

Each tiny tadpole

Each apple and pear
Each breath of air

Each lively stream
And quiet moonbeam

And bless each birth

In our home called Earth.